Spring

A Level Two Reader

By Cynthia Klingel and Robert B. Noyed

The Child's World®

Spring is here! Spring is a season. It comes after winter and before summer.

In spring, the cold days of winter are gone. There is more sunlight during the day. The sun makes it warmer outside.

Spring days can be cloudy. Rain falls from these clouds. The extra rain and sunlight help plants to grow.

The leaves come out on the trees. The grass turns green and grows. Flowers and plants begin to bloom.

Spring is a busy time for animals. Young animals come out into the warm sun.

Birds build their nests. Then they lay their eggs. Soon baby birds will hatch from the eggs.

Spring is a busy time for people, too. Farmers take care of the newborn animals. They plant seeds in the fields.

Children play outside in the spring. They ride their bikes. The windy days make it fun to fly kites.

18

Spring is the time for baseball. Children get out their bats and balls. The warm weather makes people want to be outside.

Winter is gone. Spring is here. Soon it will be summer.

Index

To Find Out More

Books

Fowler, Allan. *How Do You Know It's Spring?* Chicago: Children's Press, 1991.

Mason, John. *Spring Weather.* New York: Bookwright Press, 1991.

Schweninger, Ann. *Springtime.* New York: Puffin Books, 1995.

Web Sites

Athena: Earth and Space Science for K-12
http://www.athena.ivv.nasa.gov/index.html
A site dedicated to many science subjects. Includes weather topics and instructional material.

Note to Parents and Educators

Welcome to The Wonders of Reading™! These books provide text at three different levels for beginning readers to practice and strengthen their reading skills. Additionally, the use of nonfiction text provides readers the valuable opportunity to *read to learn*, not just to learn to read.

These leveled readers allow children to choose books at their level of reading confidence and performance. Level One books offer beginning readers simple language, word choice, and sentence structure as well as a word list. Level Two books feature slightly more difficult vocabulary, longer sentences, and longer total text. In the back of each Level Two book are an index and a list of books and Web sites for finding out more information. Level Three books continue to extend word choice and length of text. In the back of each Level Three book are a glossary, an index, and a list of books and Web sites for further research.

State and national standards in reading and language arts emphasize using nonfiction at all levels of reading development. The Wonders of Reading™ fill the historical void in nonfiction material for the primary grade readers with the additional benefit of a leveled text.

About the Authors

Cindy Klingel has worked as a high school English teacher and an elementary teacher. She is currently the curriculum director for a Minnesota school district. Writing children's books is another way for her to continue her passion for sharing the written word with children. Cindy Klingel is a frequent visitor to the children's section of bookstores and enjoys spending time with her many friends, family, and two daughters.

Bob Noyed started his career as a newspaper reporter. Since then, he has worked in communications and public relations for more than fourteen years for a Minnesota school district. He enjoys writing books for children and finds that it brings a different feeling of challenge and accomplishment from other writing projects. He is an avid reader who also enjoys music, theater, traveling, and spending time with his wife, son, and daughter.

Published by The Child's World®, Inc.
PO Box 326
Chanhassen, MN 55317-0326
800-599-READ
www.childsworld.com

Photo Credits
© Andy Sacks/Tony Stone Images: 13
© B.W. Hoffman/Unicorn Stock Photos: 9
© Darrell Gulin/Tony Stone Images: 2
© Don Smetzer/Tony Stone Images: 17
© Ed Harp/Unicorn Stock Photos: 6
© 1999 Gijsbert van Frankenhuyzen/Dembinsky Photo Assoc. Inc.: 21
© Glen Allison/Tony Stone Images: 14
© H. Richard Johnston/Tony Stone Images: cover
© Mark & Sue Werner/Unicorn Stock Photos: 10
© Peter Correz/Tony Stone Images: 5
© Wayne Eastep/Tony Stone Images: 18

Project Coordination: Editorial Directions, Inc.
Photo Research: Alice K. Flanagan

Library of Congress Cataloging-in-Publication Data
Klingel, Cynthia Fitterer.
Spring / by Cynthia Klingel and Robert B. Noyed.
p. cm. — (Wonder books)
Includes index.
Summary: Simple text describes the season of spring, the changes the Earth
goes through, and the effects that can be seen on plants, animals, and people.
ISBN 1-56766-813-5 (lib. reinforced)
1. Spring—Juvenile literature.   [1. Spring.]
I. Noyed, Robert B.   II. Title.   III. Wonder books (Chanhassen, Minn.)

QB637.5 .K55   2000
508.2—dc21   99-057446

24